Six Runs!

Ginn

Heinemann Educational Publishers
Halley Court, Jordan Hill, Oxford OX2 8EJ
Part of Harcourt Education

Heinemann is the registered trademark of Harcourt Education Ltd

First published 2007

10 09 08 07
10 9 8 7 6 5 4 3 2 1

British Library Cataloguing in Publication Data is available
from the British Library on request.

13-digit ISBN: 978 0 435988 73 9

Designed and typeset by Debbie Oatley @ room9design
Original illustrations © Harcourt Education Limited, 2007
Printed and bound at Scotprint, UK

Acknowledgements
The author and publishers would like to thank Nasser Khan for his invaluable assistance in the development of this book.

Harcourt would like to thank BGT&T for its support in publishing this series.

Series Editors: Diane Browne (fiction)
Nasser Khan (non-fiction)

Six Runs!

by

Diane Browne

David was playing really well. He saw the ball coming down towards the wicket. It seemed as big as a football. He couldn't miss it. Pow! It connected with his bat. Six runs for sure!

David watched it as the ball soared over the edge of the playground. That was one way to get a six – the best way! It went over the mango tree. That was another way to get a six.

He wished it into Mrs. Grant's garden. He wished that ball with all his might into Mrs. Grant's garden. He knew his friends were wishing the same thing.

Crash! That was not Mrs. Grant's garden. That was a window!

All the children on the field shouted as if with one voice. "Run! Run!" And they ran. The boy who owned the bat had run half way across the field when he suddenly turned and ran back.

He turned back and shouted at David. "Run man! What happen to you? Run!" But David stood rooted to the spot. It was his ball.

However, he was sure that wasn't why he couldn't move. It was something his father and grandfather had taught him. You couldn't run away from trouble. You had to face it like a man. And he was in big trouble.

He was supposed to have gone straight home. Then there was the window. Perhaps it was not just any window that was broken. Perhaps it was a window of the Singh's house!

Well, maybe Mr. Singh was there? He would understand. No, he would be at work. Maybe Mrs. Singh, their teacher?

No, he had seen her marking some papers when he and the boys had gone across the field.

So it could only be... well, maybe he wasn't at home. The other boys had all disappeared and he hadn't heard any other sound since the terrible crash.

Then a loud voice shouted, "What happen here! What happen here!"

He knew who it was, although he had never heard the voice before. It was an old voice, a strong, old voice. David stood there waiting for his doom. He wanted to run, but it was too late.

David knew that to be seen running away was even worse than breaking the window. He did not feel much like a man.

A face appeared over the fence which separated the playing field from the houses behind it. Yes, it must be old Mr. Singh. David's family and the Singhs were friends, had always been friends. However, his grandfather and Mr. Singh were not. They had been friends once, but something had happened.

David's grandfather and Mr. Singh had not spoken to each other for years. To break a window was bad. But even worse was when that house was the home of the person that his grandfather was not talking with!

"You, boy!" the man shouted. "This your ball?"

David thought that he must have nodded his head, but he was so frightened that he didn't think he could move any part of him. "Come here, boy!"

David found that he could move after all. He walked across the field towards the old man.

"Meet me round the front!" By that the man meant David should walk the length of the fence to the part where it met the road. David walked quickly. He half thought that maybe Mr. Singh wouldn't be waiting there, but of course he was.

Mr. Singh stood with the ball in one hand and a walking stick in the other. Just like his grandfather, David thought. "Where are the other boys?" Mr. Singh asked. "They...they left, sir," David replied.
"You batting or bowling?" said Mr. Singh.
"Batting," mumbled David.
"What's your name boy," Mr. Singh said.

"David...David Grant." David knew, this was it now. Maybe Mr. Singh didn't know who he was before, but now he knew.

"Grant! Emmanuel Grant's grandson?" Mr. Singh's face had become dark and angry like the sky before it is going to rain. David nodded. For a moment Mr. Singh hesitated, then he shouted, "Follow me!"

“We’re going to your house right now. We’re going to see about this. Windows cost money.”

David followed Mr. Singh along the road. Mr. Singh's house was at the end of the road, so they had to pass all the other houses. People looked out of their windows. People looked over their fences.

David wondered if his friends were somewhere hiding, peeping out from their hiding places and seeing his embarrassment and fright. Because he was frightened. What if his grandfather was at home?

His father was at work. His mother was at the hospital where she worked as a nurse.

Of course, his grandfather was at home. That was why he was supposed to have gone home right after school! His grandfather had been sick. He was much better now, but his parents still wanted David to stay with him.

They were at his house.

Mr. Singh hammered loudly with his fist on the metal postbox on the gate. David opened the gate. At the same time the front door opened and his grandfather stood there, leaning on his stick. The two old men glared at each other across the short distance of the yard between the gate and the house.

"This your grandson?" shouted Mr. Singh.

"Yes, he is," David's grandfather shouted back.

David wondered if two old men with walking sticks could have a fight.

"He break my window with his cricket ball," shouted Mr. Singh.

"He hit a six then!" David's grandfather shouted back.

There was silence. Then to David's surprise, Mr. Singh started to laugh. "Yes, man, he did. He hit a six. Just like you did when you break the window in my father's house."

David's grandfather was laughing too. "Yes, man. How you remember that? That was so long ago and I was in so much trouble."

"Me too," said Mr. Singh.

By this time Mr. Singh was up to the front door. David followed slowly, because he didn't understand what was happening. "So why we not talking again?" said Mr. Singh.

"I forget," said David's grandfather.

By this time they were in the house. David wasn't really listening as they talked, because his mind was fixed on his punishment. Then he heard Mr. Singh speak.

“The other boys run away. Your grandson, stood his ground,” said Mr. Singh.

“That’s my grandson. He will take his punishment like a man.”

That was when David realized that he would still be punished by his parents. Maybe not for breaking the window, but for not going straight home like he had been told to.

The two old men were by this time sitting on some chairs in the living room and laughing and talking.

They were talking about two old time cricketers from when they were children, Ramadhin and Valentine, who had helped win a great victory for the West Indies against England.

"We never grew up to be the other Ramadhin and Valentine, eh," said David's grandfather.

"No," Mr. Singh replied. "But I tell you what.

We could show these young boys some cricket moves. We could help to build the next great West Indies team."

David didn't know if his grandfather and Mr. Singh could really turn his friends and himself into a great cricket team, but he was glad that they were friends again. And that was when he thought that maybe his parents wouldn't punish him too much after all. He had brought together two old friends. That must mean something!

Maybe they would take away his cricket ball for a week, or something like that. He knew he would lose his allowance until the window was paid for. That that was OK though. He would be able to take his punishment like a man.

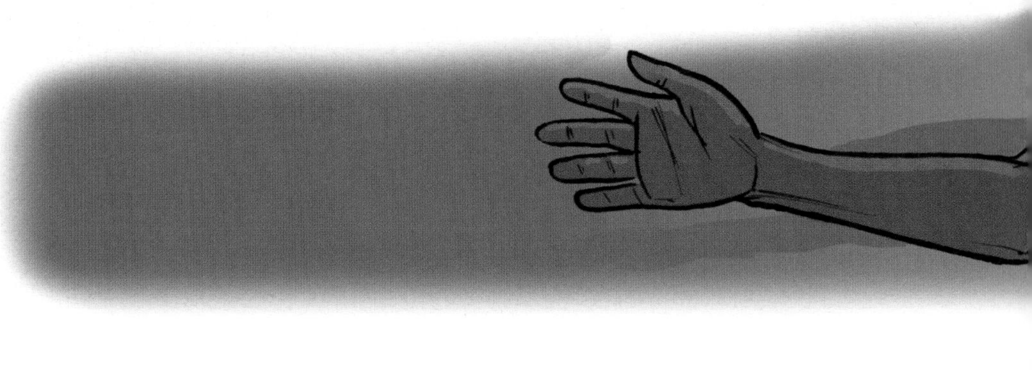

Two Tickets for the Test

by

Diane Browne

Jason rushed into the kitchen. "I've got two tickets for the Test!" he exclaimed, showing them to his mother and father. "Grandpa gave them to me. Just wait till I tell Ritchie. We can go to the Test after all!"

His mother stopped washing the lettuce in her hand. His father, who had been standing in front of the open fridge, while drinking some lemonade, slowly closed the door. There was a strange silence, a silence of surprise, and a silence of confusion. Jason didn't know how he knew this, but he just knew.

His mother was looking at him and his father was looking at his mother. What was wrong? What had he said? Why weren't they as happy as he was?

His Mum said, "You are going with Ritchie?" in a tone of total disbelief.

"We thought that you would take your brother with you," said his father quietly.

Jason stared at his parents in shock. "But Ritchie is my best friend. And we promised each other that whoever got some tickets, we'd share them with each other. What do you expect me to tell Ritchie?"

"Your grandfather gave them to you," said his Mum.

"I'm sure he would expect you to take Martin, and it would mean so much to Martin. Ritchie will understand."

"Grandpa didn't say anything like that," Jason said. "A best friend is a best friend. Martin is not my best friend; he's my little brother. I'm not going to have any fun with Martin."

"Well," said his Mum, "If you don't take Martin, you don't go. I'll tell your grandfather. I'm sure he'll understand."

"That's not fair!" said Jason, "I don't want to go with Martin!"

Suddenly, Jason noticed that his parents were very still. What had happened? He soon found out. Martin had come into the kitchen while he was talking.

Martin stood there. He was only a year younger than Jason, but something had happened to him when he was being born and now he wore a leg brace on one leg.

Everybody said he would be okay by the time he was grown up. For now he walked with a limp.

“Its okay, Jason,” Martin said. “I don’t mind if I don’t go. Ritchie is your best friend and you promised him.”

Jason felt so bad. Martin wanted to be his best friend but Ritchie was his best friend. Martin didn't have any boys to be his best friend, because he couldn't play sports.

Martin's best friend was Charlene from next door. They would read books and use the computer together. The worst thing was he knew Martin really wanted to go to the test match. He had been talking about it.

Jason hoped that his parents did not think that he didn't want to be seen with Martin at the test. He especially hoped that Martin didn't think that was it. Jason usually liked spending time with Martin – but for this exciting trip, he wanted to go with his best friend, not have to babysit his younger brother!

In his heart he knew that wasn't it. He had promised his best friend. How could parents expect you to take your little brother to something as big as a test match instead of your friend? Martin and he couldn't even have a conversation about the game. He and Ritchie could jump up and shout when there was a six. Martin couldn't do that. How could he enjoy the test if he couldn't do those things? What would Ritchie think if he took Martin instead of him?

No, he would not go with Martin instead of Ritchie. He couldn't! The next few days were difficult ones for Jason.

His parents were determined that he would not be going to the test without his brother. Martin, who was always so nice, was even nicer now. He kept saying that he understood, and that he didn't want to go. It seemed to Jason that, to prove that he didn't need his brother as his best friend, Martin spent extra time on the computer with Charlene.

The test was only a week away and nothing had changed. He wanted to tell his parents they were only behaving like that because of his brother's disability but he was afraid to do that. He didn't know what would happen. Jason could not believe that he might really not go to the test.

Jason told Ritchie about the whole thing. Ritchie said he understood, but Jason could see that he didn't really.

Jason thought of appealing to his grandfather, but he knew his mother had already talked to him. Besides, his grandfather always said that he did not interfere in the way their parents brought up him and Martin.

Then suddenly, like a bolt of lightning, it was solved! Ritchie had an uncle who had got tickets for a lot of people, and two had decided not to go. Ritchie's uncle had given the extra tickets to Ritchie.

Jason could hardly believe his good luck. They were both going to the test after all!

He told his parents at dinner that very night.

“Lovely!” said his mother. “So now you can give the two tickets you got from Grandpa to Martin and Charlene. I’m sure you would like to go, wouldn’t you, Martin?”

Martin’s face was radiant with delight, as he nodded his head. Jason was pleased that it had worked out so well for all of them. He hadn’t enjoyed upsetting Martin.

Then his father said firmly, "And Martin and Charlene can go along with you and Ritchie. They are too young to be by themselves. Go early so that you can get four seats together."

Jason didn't know how he didn't fall off his chair in shock! One minute everything was rosy, with a great test to enjoy with all the other boys from school who were lucky enough to get tickets. The next minute you had your little brother and a girl with you.

Jason saw the look on his father's face. He nodded his head glumly. Of course Martin was being nice again and saying, once they got in, he and Charlene didn't have to sit with them. Jason knew that he couldn't argue with his parents this time. Ritchie didn't seem to mind when he told him. At least, if he did, he didn't show it.

On the day of the test, they were early. They got four seats together.

The other boys they had planned to meet joined them one by one or two by two. Jason could see the surprise on some of their faces when they saw not only Martin, but also Charlene. He was at the test match but it was ruined before it even began.

The first shock for Jason was when he discovered that Martin and Charlene knew not only the names of the players, but also the batting order. Martin jumped up and down just like everybody else for each six. Charlene knew all the positions on the field. She and Martin discussed the strategy of the opposing team's captain as he placed his fielders. Charlene and Martin were shouting advice to the batsmen, just like everybody else. Jason almost forgot he was with his little brother and a girl.

When the first West Indies wicket fell, leg before wicket, Charlene assured everybody that the playback would show that the umpire had made a mistake. And she was right. When the second one went, caught behind the wicket, Martin offered to go and play for the West Indies right away if they needed him. Jason couldn't believe it! Martin and Charlene were just like everybody else in the stands.

The next shock was when both Martin and Charlene began to give information on cricket matches that had taken place before. It wasn't like they were showing off either. It just fitted into the conversation. One or the other could tell the batsmen that if they wanted to make a century like so and so in some famous match, they had to make a particular stroke.

Or if they didn't want to be out like so and so, they had to be careful of the bowler, and so on. Everybody, even grown-ups, were enjoying Martin and Charlene's comments.

One man turned towards Charlene. "Little lady, maybe you should manage the West Indies Team," he said.

“That’s exactly what I’m going to do when I grow up,” she said. “And then you are going to see how things turn out.”

The man chuckled and said he believed her.

Then the man said to Martin. "And what are you going to do, son? I know you are going to be on the team."

Jason felt sorry for his brother. He hadn't realized how much his brother loved cricket. Martin could never play though, and now he would be embarrassed by the man's question.

Martin replied with a grin, "I'm going to be a batsman. I can't be a bowler because of my leg, you know. But by the time I'm grown up, it will be fine. It will be strong enough for me to run between the wickets. Charlene and I go on the Internet all the time. We know everything there is to know about cricket. I know every stroke there is and how to play every ball. I am going to be a great batsman."

Charlene was nodding her head furiously in agreement, and a number of grown-ups near by were also nodding their heads in approval.

And that was how Jason found out how much cricket meant to his little brother. He also found, to his surprise, that he believed that his brother would one day be a great batsman.

The Challenge Match

by

Hazel D. Campbell

As soon as Miss Thompson left the room, the quarrel between the boys and girls in the class exploded. The boys had been boasting about their recent cricket win. The girls had won the class spelling bee for the fourth week in a row and didn't see why the boys should have all the glory.

The boys were feeling ashamed. They told themselves the girls were cheating, but they couldn't prove this. Instead they were mocking the girls' victory. This just made the girls even more cross!

“Cheaters!” “Duncie” and other taunts flew across the room until class prefect, Ashley, yelled: “Quiet!”

Ashley was the smallest girl in the class, but she had the loudest voice. According to the boys, her mouth was the biggest part of her body.

The intense rivalry between the boys and girls in that school had to do with the principal, Mr. Smellie, who had some old-fashioned ideas about what boys and girls should do. He didn't allow the boys to do home economics and the girls could not play football and cricket.

Girls sat on one side of the classroom and boys on the other. Today, smarting from the girls' spelling bee victory and their taunts, the boys threw out the one challenge they were certain they could win.

Craig, the leader of the boys' group, said, "Since you think you are so good, I challenge you to play the boys in a cricket match. Let's see how good you are."

Shocked silence greeted this challenge. As they all knew, girls were not allowed to play cricket. After the first surprise, the boys, knowing they would win any such match, began to chant: "Yes! Play us, if you think you are so good."

"Time out!" shouted Ashley. "We need to discuss this." For a few minutes there was intense whispering on both sides of the room. "Okay," Ashley announced, "we will play you."

The boys laughed. This was too easy. "Okay," Craig agreed. "Tomorrow after school, the other teachers will think we got Smellie's permission to use the far field."

"Just one more thing," Ashley said. Her voice was uncharacteristically soft and sweet. "If we win the match, the boys will have to play a game of netball – in the netball uniform."

Laughter and jeers erupted in the room. "As if that will ever happen," Craig said softly.

Then he raised his voice: "And when we beat you, you have to help us to win the next spelling bee."

"Yeah! Yeah!" the girls replied.

After school, the girls held a serious meeting to discuss the possibilities.

“Why you take them on?” wailed Shadee. “We don’t know anything about playing cricket. We are bound to lose.”

“We have all of this evening to find out how to play the game and get a little practice,” Ashley assured her.

"You think it is that easy?" asked Meena. She had only recently started coming to that school. "I help my brother practise his batting and it takes a long time to get good at it."

"Well! Well!" said Ashley. "We have at least one person who can play cricket."

"I never play a match. When he can't find anybody else, he forces me to bowl, so he can practise his batting," Meena replied.

"Good enough," Ashley said. "The rest of you ask your fathers and your brothers how to play the game and if you can get them to give you a little practise this evening, do it. Those boys are clowns. They shouldn't be too hard to beat."

In school, every chance the girls got to talk they spent sharing what they had learned about the game. They were swapping cricket terms like silly mid-on, silly mid-off, square leg, boundary, slips and gullies. Few of them understood what they were talking about.

Finally, Ashley said, “All we really need to know is that when we are batting, we mustn’t let the ball hit the wicket. We must hit the ball hard to get a four or a six. We must run fast when somebody hits the ball so we can reach the other wicket. And when we are fielding we must try to catch every ball they hit, or try to run them out – simple.”

The girls took turns getting the feel of the cricket bat which Meena had borrowed from her brother. Some of them were holding a cricket bat for the very first time.

Then Ashley named the team:
Ashley, who would be the captain;
Meena, who had the most experience;
Shadee, who had a cousin who played national cricket;
Brenda, who thought she knew something about the game;
Bianca, because she was Ashley's best friend, and Chandra because she was the only one to volunteer.

The boys had no trouble making up their team.

All of them played cricket as part of the school's games programme. These were the ones chosen for this historic game: Craig as the captain with the rest of the team as Nandi, Sanjay, Brian, Spunks and David.

As soon as the last bell rang, there was a rush for the far playing field.

The boys looked at the girls who had come out to play and sniggered. There was no doubt about who would win this match.

They tossed a coin. The boys won and sent the girls in to bat first.

Ashley faced the first ball. Spunks was the wicket-keeper, and confidently took his place behind the stump. Sanjay was the first bowler for the boys. With a smile he waved at the boys watching, who cheered. Then he turned, ran up and bowled. Ashley never even saw the ball. All she heard was a swish past her and the shouts of the children, "Clean bowled!"

When she looked around, her middle stump was lying flat on the ground.

Ashley walked away dejected as the boys sang, "Nought for one. Let's make it nought for two!"

There was much laughter among the boys, and many groans from the girls. It didn't get any better for them.

Chandra was also cleaned bowled; Meena run out; Brenda caught; Shadee out LBW (none of the girls knew what that meant) and Bianca never even got a chance to bat.

At the end of their session the girls had made only 15 runs. It looked as if it was going to be a short match. It wouldn't take the boys too long to better that score. The girls watching groaned.

The only one on the girls' team who had any idea of how to bowl was Meena, so they put her on. Ashley passed her the ball.

First ball to Craig, he hit it to the boundary – four runs. Already they only needed 12 more to win.

Craig grinned as he watched the ball fly away, Bianca running after it. He could get these runs alone, easy as pie, Craig thought, smugly.

"Tighten your field," some boys shouted mocking instructions to the girls. "Get closer." There was laughter all round – some of the boys on the team joined in as well.

Then suddenly, Meena's next ball bowled Craig. He couldn't believe it. Neither could Meena.

There was a sudden silence before, for the first time, the girls started screaming encouragement to their team.

The boys became quieter and quieter as the match progressed. Nandi was caught by Brenda, who was good at netball. Meena clean bowled David and Brian. Finally, only Sanjay and Spunks were left to bat. The boys had made 13 runs. This pair needed to make only 3 runs to win the match, but Meena was such a good bowler, the girls could win the match.

Silence descended on the field as a now confident Meena, wiped the ball on her shorts.

Then, with a swish the ball flew from her hand. Spunks hit it as hard as he could. The ball flew off towards the boundary. Both boys and girls were shouting as they watched the ball roll towards the boundary.

The excitement was so intense that they failed to recognise the adult male figure walking rapidly towards them until he swooped down on the ball and picked it up.

Ashley nearly collided with him. Then she nearly fainted.

A brief, awful silence blanketed the field. Then, with a cry, the children started scampering away, “Smellie! Smellie come!”

The players didn’t run. They knew it was useless trying to escape from the headmaster. Mr. Smellie stood throwing the ball up in the air and catching it. He seemed to be thinking.

“Come here all of you!” he commanded. The two teams fearfully drew near. “You all know that rule breakers must be punished,” he said. The children nodded. They had no excuses. “Report to my office tomorrow morning.”

Then Mr. Smellie continued, "I was watching you play. Maybe I should re-consider my ban against girls playing cricket." There was a faint smile on his face.

What a match! Spunks had made two runs, but Ashley had been centimetres away from stopping the ball, so they agreed on a draw. Cricket has a way of evening out the odds.